SHOW AND TELL

SHOW AND TE

ADAM

BETTY

CHARLIE

DARCY

GEORGE

Written and illustrated by
Rob Biddulph

HOLLY

ISAAC

JESSIE

HarperCollins *Children's Books*

First published in hardback in Great Britain by
HarperCollins Children's Books in 2019
First published in paperback in 2020
1 3 5 7 9 10 8 6 4 2
ISBN: 978-0-00-831803-1

HarperCollins Children's Books is a division
of HarperCollins Publishers Ltd.
Text and illustrations copyright © Rob Biddulph 2019
The author/illustrator asserts the moral right to be
identified as the author/illustrator of the work.
A CIP catalogue record for this book is available
from the British Library. All rights reserved.

Visit our website at www.harpercollins.co.uk

Printed and bound in China

EDDIE

FLORENCE

KENZO

LILY

MO

NELLY

FIVE THINGS TO FIND IN THIS BOOK

1. An explorer's pith helmet ☐
2. Some Liquorice Allsorts ☐
3. A game of cat and mouse ☐
4. A pencil sharpener ☐
5. A hidden A to Z ☐

OLIVER

PARMIDA

QUINN

REBECCA

SILVIO

THEA

For the staff and pupils of
St Mary's School, Finchley

ULYSSES

VIOLET

WILLIAM

XANTHE

YAO

Meet
Class 2L.
These
kids are
excited.

Meet Mr Lumsden. He is their teacher,
A giant moustache his most prominent feature.
"Remember," he says with a smile in his eyes,

"The child that impresses
me most wins a prize."

A hush fills the classroom.
It's time to begin.
"Adam, you're first.
Show us what
you've brought in."

"Well," says the boy,
"I have treasure, indeed.
A small piece of sunshine,
this sunflower seed."

"A sunflower seed?
That's so BORING!"
shouts Betty.
"I've got a whole tin of
bright blue spaghetti."

"I think you'll agree that
mine beats yours, hands down.
That seed is so tiny.
And boring. And brown."

"Blue pasta?" says Charlie.
"I guess it's okay.
But my hat's the best thing
that you'll see today."

"Nonsense!" says Darcy.
"My gold violins
are far more impressive!"

And so it
begins...

From Eddie, SNAP! SNAP!
Venus flytraps. One bunch.

From Florence, a sandwich
she's brought in for lunch.

George has a set of
his grandad's false teeth.

And Holly, a jolly red
robot called Keith.

From Isaac,
a painting.

From Jessie,
a stamp.

From Kenzo,
these feathers.

From Lily,
this lamp.

Mo has a
laser sword.

Nelly,
a carrot.

Here's Oliver's
spacesuit.

And Parmida's
parrot.

Quite an impressive collection so far.
But wait. Turn the page. We are raising the bar...

Here's the new leader. It's Quinn, by a distance. He's brought in the speediest car in existence!

But hold on a second,
cos two minutes later
Rebecca walks in
with her pet alligator!

Oh, my! Look what Silvio found in the park!

And who's this with Thea? The Queen of Denmark!

Then our friend Ulysses enters the room,
With monster in tow (from Loch Ness, I assume).

Looks like this card is
the ace in the pack...

...Till Violet appears

with Big Ben on her back.

Give it up, folks! A big hand for the winner...

But no!

William makes her
look like a beginner!

Can he be beaten?
The next person may know...

It's Xanthe,
and she's got a red hot

VOI

CANO!

The champion!

Wait! Have we spoken too soon?
Cos Yao's just arrived...

And he's holding... the MOON!

Darkness.

A total eclipse of the sun.

Yao's moony moment
has stopped all the fun.

But look! Bringing light to the end of our story,

it's Zorg the Explorer, from Alpha Centauri.

Zorg gathers the flytraps... the robot... the parrot...
The car... and the feathers... the painting... the carrot...
The monster... the sandwich... the spacesuit... Big Ben...
He ties them all on to his spaceship, and then...

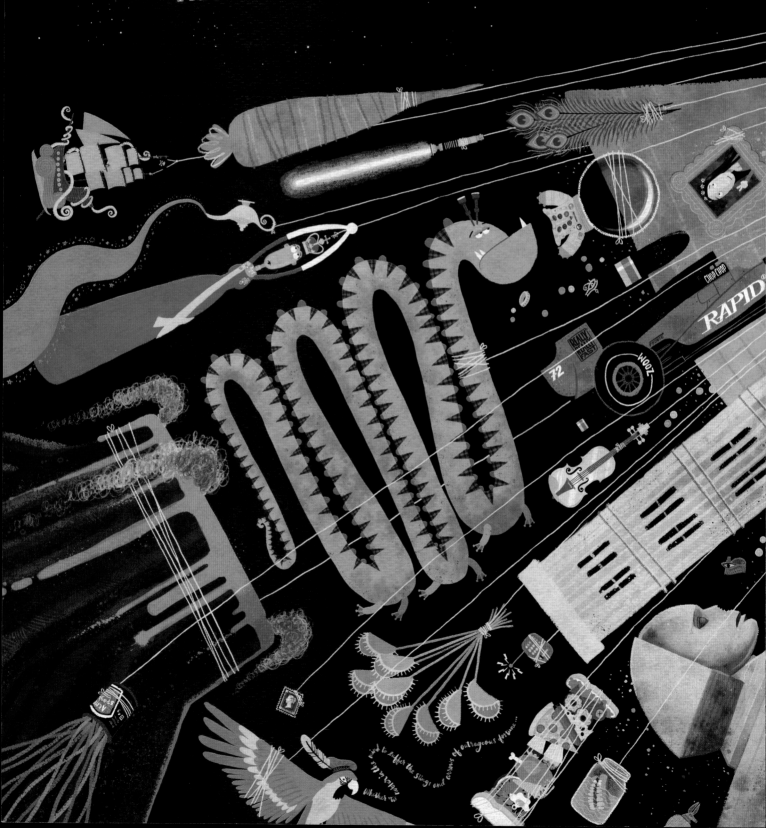

...He tows them away
to a cosmic museum.
They're on display now
if you'd like to go see 'em.

Back in the classroom it's quiet, indeed.
The only thing left? Adam's sunflower seed.

And so Mr Lumsden,
a smile in his eyes,
Walks over to Adam
and hands him the prize.

"This seed," says the teacher, "is certainly tiny.
It looks pretty boring – not flashy or shiny."

"But," he explains as he kneels down beside it,
"Like all the best things..."

"...it has magic inside it."